W9-AMO-662

Monday
AИИe Herbauts

ENCHANTED LION BOOKS
New York

Monday is his name.

Monday awaits Tuesday.
On Tuesday he thinks about Wednesday,
on Wednesday he feels so small,
so very small that by Thursday
he no longer knows if
tomorrow will really be Friday.
On Saturday, he is astonished.
Sunday passes in silence.

Hello, Monday!

Hello, Lester Day!

What would you say to a cup of tea,
one sugar and two spoons?

Hello, Monday!

Hello, Tom Morrow!

I have come to say good day.

Our three friends
sit in front
of their grand piano.

Lester Day plays backwards,
Tom Morrow plays wonderfully well
and Monday is just delighted.

They play for a long time.
They have the time.

Good night!

Good evening, Monday!

I am Spring.
I am green, I abound.

Into the wind I put its rustling sound.
I quiver, timid in the pinkness of a bud.

I am tender, impatient, and eagerly awaited.
I expand myself from leaves to blooms
and fill the sky where my laughter booms.

Salutations! I am Summer.
Through the still, golden wheat I make my way,
while yet I stay, awaiting full ripening.
I watch colors deepen as fragrances thicken and intensify.
Content, I continue the light of midday through
the hours, as the shadows steal away, afraid.

I am wild **Autumn!**

I turn,

I burn,

I blow *and whirl.*

Red and brown, I confound.
I surprise, I disguise, I fade away,

I fly, I flee!

My name is **Winter.**
My country goes white with cold and silence.
Formed of frost, my stars shiver.
Time is unmoving, when suddenly
the wind whips up
with ice and **snow.**

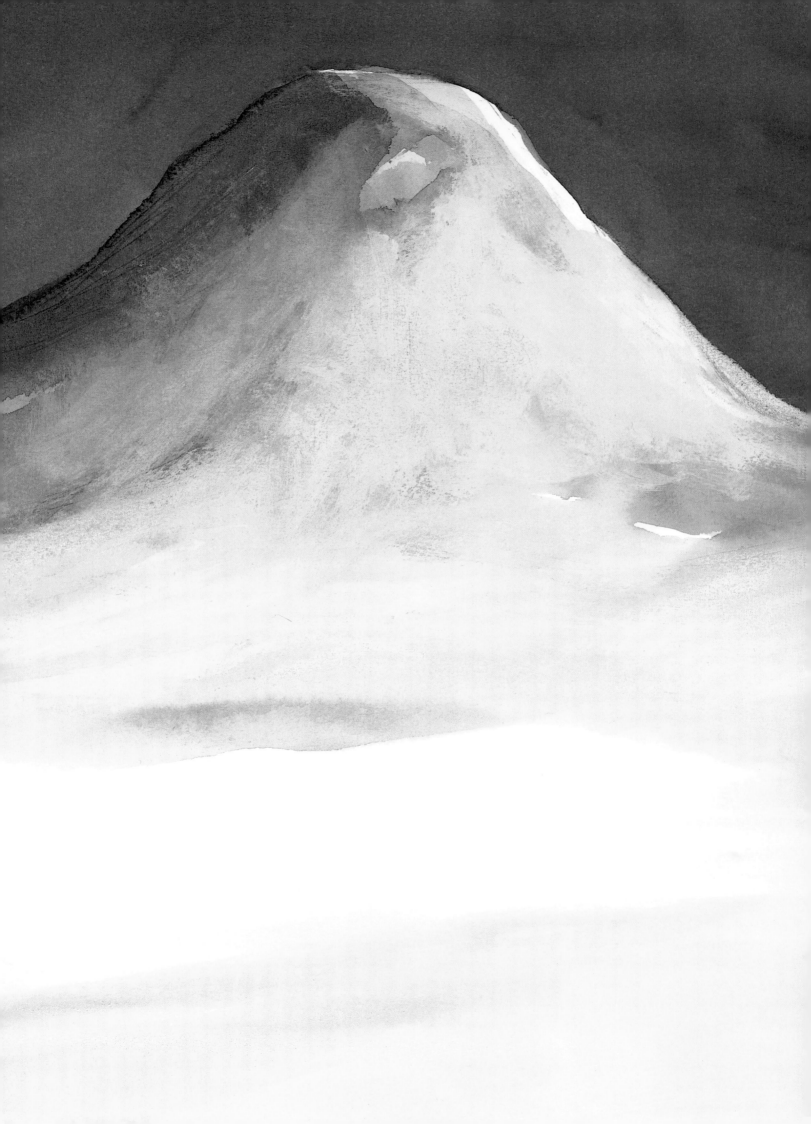

Monday?

Monday?

Do you remember Monday?
He waited for Lester Day
and thought about Tom Morrow.
He felt so small, so very small
that he knew almost nothing
about Thursday
or Friday.
On Saturday he smiled dreamily.
Sunday passed in silence.

And the following Monday
comes,
albeit a little different...

Monday is his name.

First American Edition published in 2006 by
Enchanted Lion Books
45 Main Street, Suite 519
Brooklyn, NY 11201

Originally published in French as *Lundi* in 2004 by Casterman, Belgium

© Casterman 2004
Translation Copyright © 2006 by Enchanted Lion Books

For information about permissions to reproduce selections
from this book, write to:
Permissions, Enchanted Lion Books,
45 Main Street, Suite 519,
Brooklyn, NY 11201

[A CIP record is on file with the Library of Congress]

ISBN 1-59270-057-8

Designer: Anne Quévy, Plume production

Printed in China

2 4 6 8 10 9 7 5 3 1

A graduate of the Academy of Fine Arts in Brussels, Auue Herbauts is a prolific and critically acclaimed author/illustrator.
Herbauts has well over twenty books to her name, many of which have been widely translated. She divides her time
between Belgium and France.